The Apple Tree

Om KIDZ
An imprint of Om Books International

First Published in 2023

Om KIDZ | Om Books International

Corporate & Editorial Office
A-12, Sector 64, Noida 201 301
Uttar Pradesh, India
Phone: +91 120 477 4100
Email: editorial@ombooks.com
Website: www.ombooksinternational.com

Sales Office
107, Ansari Road, Darya Ganj
New Delhi 110 002, India
Phone: +91 11 4000 9000
Email: sales@ombooks.com

ISBN: 978-93-94547-18-6

Printed in India

10 9 8 7 6 5 4 3 2 1

The Apple Tree

I'm all set to read

Paste your photograph here

My name is

There was a beautiful **apple tree** in the **park**.
It had big red **apples** hanging **from** it.

Liz wanted to eat one of the **apples**. She **jumped** and **jumped**.

But she **could** not
reach the **apples**.

She **called** her **brother** Hans
to help her get the **apples**.
Hans was taller **than** Liz.
He **jumped** and **jumped**.

But he **could** not reach
the **apples**.

Hans **called** his best **friend** Manny. Manny was a bit taller **than** Hans. Hans asked, "Manny, can you **pluck some** apples for us?"

Manny **jumped**
and **jumped**!
But he **could** not
pluck an **apple**.

Liz, Hans and Manny stood sadly under the **tree looking** at the hanging **apples**. “What should we do?” asked Manny.

Hans looked **around**. He saw a **gardener walking** with a small **ladder** in his hand.

"Look! The **gardener** has a **ladder**," **said** Hans.
"Let us ask him for help."

The **children** ran to the **gardener**. "Hello!" **said** Hans excitedly. The **gardener** looked at him in surprise.

“Can you **climb** up the **apple tree with your ladder**? We **want** to eat **some** of the **apples.**”

But the ladder was too **small**. The gardener could not **help** them.

Then along came Big Jim. He **plucked** an **apple from** the tree and started **eating** it!

He **looked** down.
He saw three **children**
and a **gardener looking**
at him hungrily.

Big Jim **plucked some apples**.

He gave three **apples** to Liz, Hans, Manny and one to the **gardener**.

Now everyone was happy.

Know Your Words

Sight Words

around	from	than	want
called	said	then	with
could	some	there	your

Naming Words

apple	friend	park
brother	gardener	tree
children	ladder	

Doing Words

called	jumped	walking
climb	looking	
eating	pluck	